# WALKING THROUGH
# THE JUNGLE

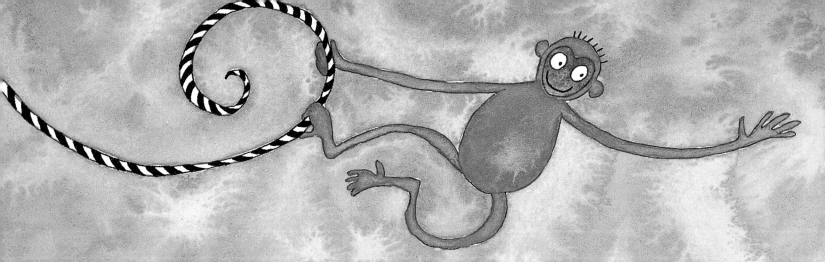

Barefoot Beginners
an imprint of
Barefoot Books Ltd
PO Box 95
Kingswood
Bristol BS30 5BH

Graphic design by Tom Grzelinski, Bath
Printed and bound in Singapore by Tien Wah Press (Pte) Ltd

This book was printed on 100% acid-free paper

Hardback ISBN 1 898000 61 1
Paperback ISBN 1 901223 76 0

British Cataloguing-in-Publication Data: a catalogue record for this book
is available from the British Library

5 7 9 8 6 4

# WALKING THROUGH THE JUNGLE

Illustrated by Debbie Harter

BAREFOOT BOOKS
BATH

Walking through the jungle,
Walking through the jungle,

What do you see?
What do you see?

Chasing after me,
Chasing after me.

Floating on the ocean,
Floating on the ocean,

What do you see?
What do you see?

Chasing after me,
Chasing after me.

Climbing in the mountains,
Climbing in the mountains,

What do you see?
What do you see?

Chasing after me,
Chasing after me.

Swimming in the river,
Swimming in the river,

What do you see?
What do you see?

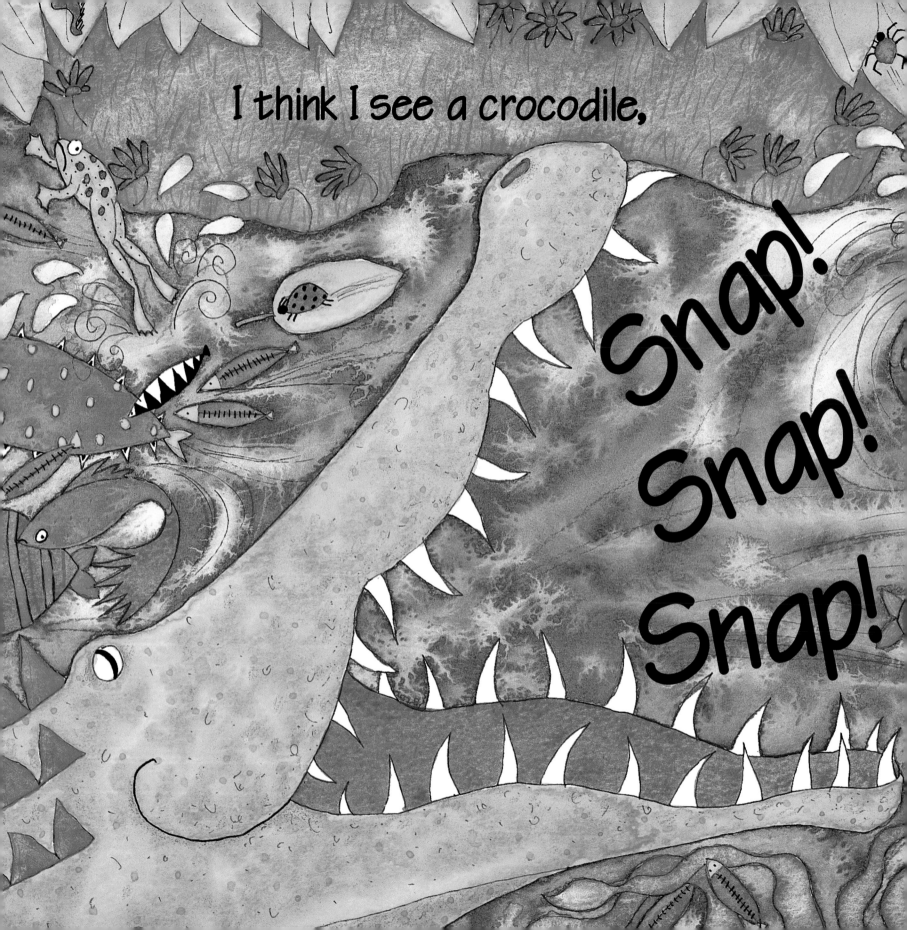

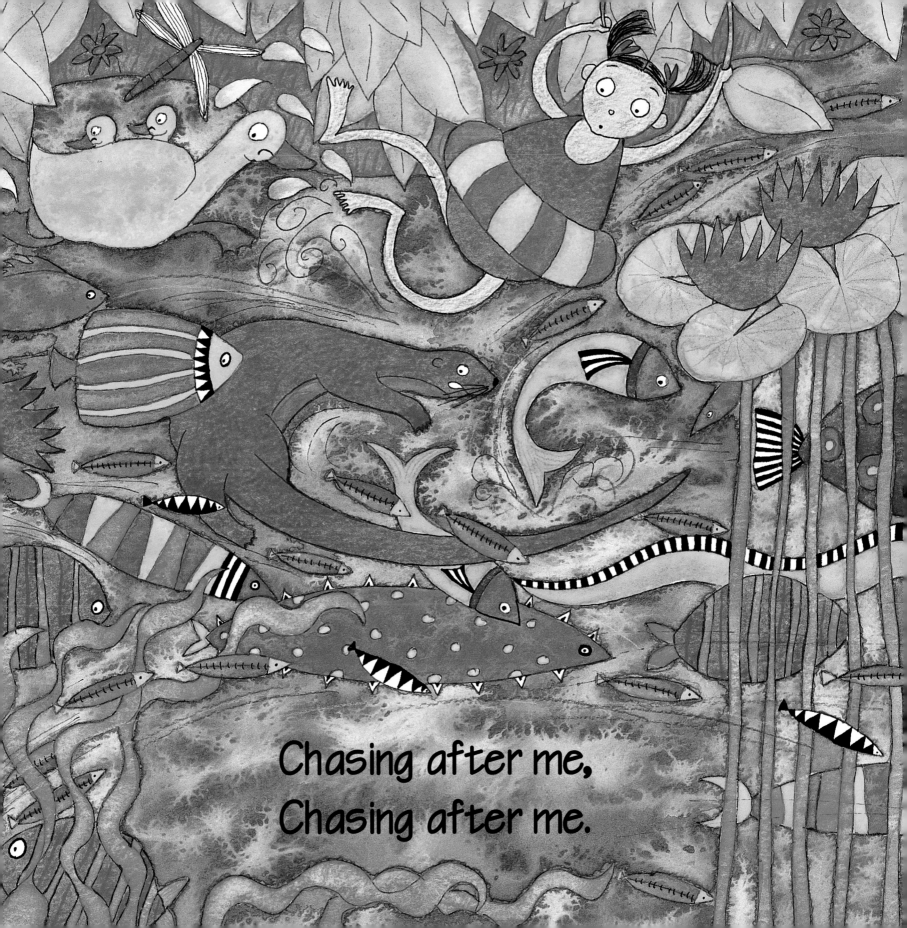

Chasing after me,
Chasing after me.

Trekking in the desert,
Trekking in the desert,

What do you see?
What do you see?

Chasing after me,
Chasing after me.

Slipping on the iceberg,
Slipping on the iceberg,

What do you see?
What do you see?

Chasing after me,
Chasing after me.

Running home for supper,
Running home for supper,

Where have you been?
Where have you been?

I've been around the world and back,
I've been around the world and back,

And guess what I've seen,
And guess what I've seen.